HANS CHRISTIAN ANDERSEN
The Wild Swans

Pictures by SUSAN JEFFERS

Retold by Amy Ehrlich

The Dial Press
New York

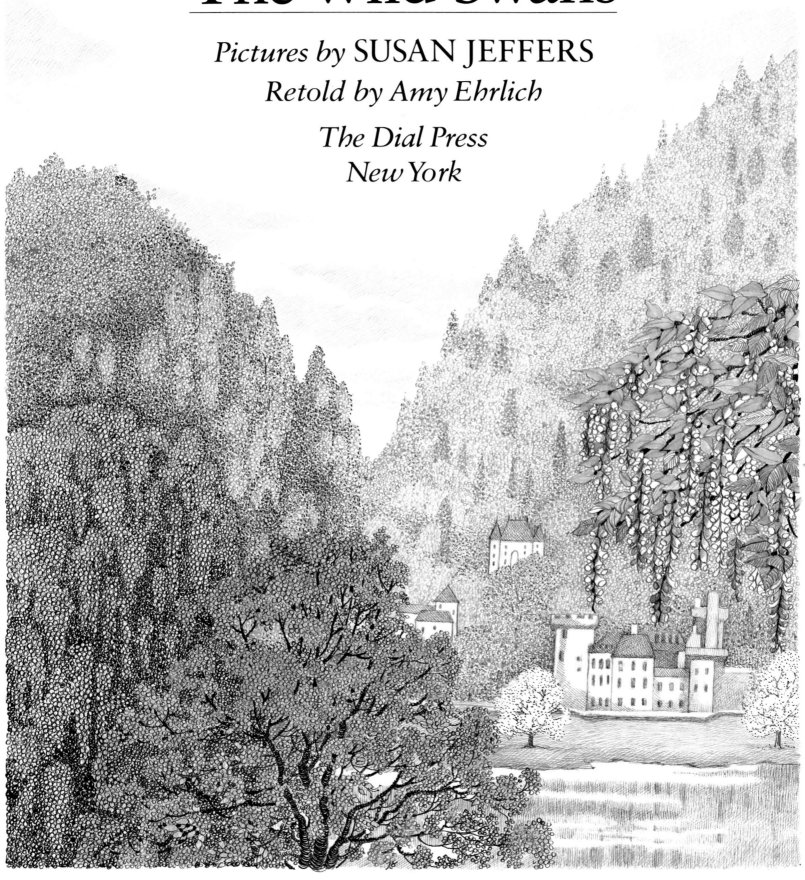

Published by
The Dial Press
1 Dag Hammarskjold Plaza
New York, New York 10017

Library of Congress Cataloging in Publication Data
Ehrlich, Amy, 1942–   The wild swans.
Summary / Eleven brothers, turned into wild swans by an evil stepmother,
are saved by the sacrifices of their beautiful sister, Elise.
[1. Fairy tales] I. Jeffers, Susan.
II. Andersen, H. C. (Hans Christian), 1805–1875. Vilde svaner.
III. Title.
PZ8.E32Wi   [E]   81-65843
ISBN 0-8037-9381-2   AACR2
ISBN 0-8037-9391-X (lib. bdg.)

The full-color artwork was prepared using a fine-line pen with ink and dyes.
They were applied over a detailed pencil drawing that was then erased.
The artwork was separated by Rainbows Inc.
The book was printed by Holyoke Lithograph Co., Inc.,
and bound by Economy Bookbinding Corporation.

For my three nephews, Chris, Gregory, and
Matthew, who are a great joy in my life

Far, far away, in a warm and pleasant land, there once lived a king who had eleven sons and one daughter. The princes wore stars on their shirts and swords at their sides, and their sister, Elise, sat on a footstool made of glass. These children were happy from the time they woke in the morning until they went to their beds at night. They never imagined another life.

But after some years had passed, the king married a wicked queen who hated the children and wanted only to be rid of them. During the wedding party she gave them no cakes or baked apples to eat; all they were allowed was a bit of sand in a teacup.

It was not long before the queen sent Elise away to be looked after by some farmers. But the fate of the princes was still more severe. "You shall become great voiceless birds and fly out into the world," she commanded.

At once the princes turned into eleven wild swans. Uttering strange and mournful cries, they flew from the palace windows and circled the countryside until they came to the place where Elise lived.

They hovered over the roof, turning their long necks and beating their wings, but by the time Elise came outside, they had gone. She stood there alone, playing with a green leaf, the one toy she had. When she held it up to the sun, it seemed to her she could see her brothers' bright eyes.

The years went by, one just like another. At the age of fifteen Elise was brought home, but when the wicked queen saw how beautiful the girl had become, she determined to have her banished forever.

Early in the morning the queen went into her marble bath and took three toads and kissed them. "Sit upon her and make her so ugly and evil that her father will not know her," she said. Then she bade Elise go for her bath. As the girl plunged into the water the first toad grasped her hair, the second her forehead, and the third her breasts. But when she arose, they had become three red poppies, for she was too good and too innocent for witchcraft to have any power.

The queen was in a rage. She ripped Elise's clothes and tangled her lovely hair and rubbed a foul ointment on her face. Then she called the king.

Horrified at her appearance, he declared she was not his daughter. No one in the palace knew her except the watchdog and the swallows, but they of course could say nothing.

Elise stole away and wandered over the fields and hills. Tears streamed down her face as she thought of her brothers, and she resolved to find them, though it might take all her life.

At nightfall she came into a great forest. The air was still and mild, and everywhere glowworms shone with a green fire. As she lay down they cascaded upon her like shooting stars. All night long Elise dreamed of her brothers. Once more they were children playing together, carefree and loved.

But when she awoke, she was alone in the forest and the sun was already high. She washed her face in a woodland pond and then set out again, without knowing where she was bound. But she had walked only a few steps when she met an old woman carrying a basket of berries. Elise asked if she had seen eleven princes riding through the forest.

"No," said the old woman, "but earlier I saw eleven swans with golden crowns swimming down a stream nearby." She pointed the way, and Elise followed the stream until it came out upon the open shore.

The whole immense sea lay before her, without boundary or end. It seemed to Elise that she could go no farther. A feeling of hopelessness swept over her, and she threw herself down and began to weep. Then suddenly on the sand she saw eleven swans' feathers. She tied them together and resolved to stay by the shore until the swans returned. It was very lonely, but she did not mind, for the sea changed constantly. The water reflected the colors of the sky, and when the wind rose, the waves tossed their white manes.

At last Elise looked up and saw eleven swans with golden crowns, flying toward the shore. She climbed quickly up the steep bank and hid while they alighted. But as the sun was setting, the swans' feathers vanished and there before Elise were all her eleven brothers.

She cried out loudly, for although they were greatly changed, she knew them at once. Then she ran into their arms, calling each one by name. The princes stared in wonder at their sister, who had become so tall and lovely, and they laughed and cried and held each other in the growing darkness. It was the eldest brother who told Elise their story.

"As long as the sun is in the sky we fly about as wild swans, but when night comes, we return to our human shape. That is why we must always search for solid ground at sunset, for as men we would fall from the clouds and crash to our deaths. Tomorrow we must fly away to a land across the sea. Have you the courage to come with us?"

"Yes! Take me please," cried Elise. "I cannot bear to let you go."

They spent the evening and all of that night making a net from willow bark and rushes. Elise lay down upon it and soon fell asleep, for it was soft as well as strong. At daybreak the brothers were changed into swans again; they seized the net with their beaks and flew up into the clouds. The

hot sun shone upon Elise's face, but one of the swans flew above her, shading her with its wide wings.

They were far out over the sea when Elise awoke. She thought she was dreaming, for it felt so strange to be carried through the air. Next to her lay some red berries and a bundle of sweet roots. The youngest brother had gathered them for her; she smiled at him gratefully, for he was the one flying above her.

They soared so high that the ships below sparkled like sea gulls upon the water, but as the sun began to set, a storm suddenly came up. Thunder rolled and lightning flashed in the sky. Elise was frightened. Her brothers had told her that in the midst of the sea was a small rock where they always landed and passed the night as men. Now, because they had to carry her, they might never reach it in time.

The sun touched the rim of the sea, and Elise's heart stood still. They could not fly fast enough; surely they would fall into the waves and drown.

When the sun was nearly hidden below the water, Elise saw the little rock below. She peered over the edge of the net, willing them to fly faster, harder. The swans plunged downward. At last her feet touched solid ground, and then the sun died out like a spark at the edge of the sea. The rock seemed so very small and exposed. But her brothers were around her, and though the heavens blazed with lightning, she was no longer afraid.

At dawn the storm had ended and the swans flew away, carrying Elise in her net. As the sun rose higher she began to see pictures in the changing shapes of clouds—mountains and glaciers and shining palaces. Then at last she looked down and saw the land for which they were bound. The swans flew over cedar woods that smelled fragrant in the sunshine, and at nightfall they set her before a cavern hung with delicate green plants.

"Now we shall see what you'll dream of tonight," said the youngest brother, showing her where she was to sleep.

"If only I could dream how to set you free," Elise said, and her mind was filled with the thought. Then it seemed to her that she flew up to the palaces she had seen in the clouds. A beautiful fairy came to greet her, yet she looked just like the old woman who had told her of the wild swans.

"Your brothers can be set free," she said. "But the anguish you must endure is great. Look well at the stinging nettle in my hand. Gather only this kind and those that grow on the graves in churchyards. They will blister your skin, but you must crush them. Spin the flax and knit it into eleven tunics. When you throw these over the wild swans, the spell will be broken. But remember—from the time you begin the work until it is ended, you must be silent. The first word you speak will pierce your brothers' hearts like a sword."

The woman touched Elise's hands with the burning nettle and awakened her. There on the cavern floor was a nettle like the one in her dream. Immediately Elise left to begin her task, weeping with excitement and gratitude. She seized the nettles, and blisters rose on her delicate hands, yet she knew she could endure any pain to free her brothers. She crushed the nettles as the woman had directed and then spun the flax.

At sundown the brothers came back and were alarmed by her silence. They thought at first it was some new spell of their evil stepmother's, but when they saw Elise's hands, they understood that her work was for their sake. The youngest brother wept, and where his tears fell, Elise felt no more pain, and the burning blisters disappeared.

All the next day she sat spinning the flax and knitting the first tunic. Then hunting horns rang out and she heard the baying of hounds. Suddenly huntsmen were there, ringed around the cavern, and the most

handsome among them was the king of the country. He came toward Elise,
dazzled as if he were in a dream.

"Why are you hiding here, beautiful maiden?" he asked.

Elise shook her head, not daring to speak, for how could she risk the
lives of her brothers?

"Come with me," said the king. "You cannot stay here." Though Elise
wept, he took her on his horse and galloped off among the mountains.

In the evening the king's magnificent city lay before them.

He led her into a palace where the walls were hung with brilliant paintings and fountains splashed in courtyards. But Elise cared for none of it. Silently she allowed the women to dress her in silks and to braid jewels through her hair.

At last she was brought before the court. So glorious was her beauty that everyone bowed down before her and the king took her for his bride. Only the archbishop was unmoved. He shook his head and whispered that the forest maiden must be a witch, that she had blinded them all and beguiled the king.

Elise could think only of her brothers and the work she had been taken from so forcibly. But soon the king led her into a little chamber that had been hung with green embroideries, exactly like the cavern in the forest. The bundle of nettles and the tunic she had completed were there.

"Now you may dream that you are back in your home," said the king. "Here is the work you were doing."

As Elise was shown all these things the king saw her smile for the first time. He clasped her to him and ordered the marriage festival to begin. The lovely, speechless girl from the forest was to be queen!

Nothing the archbishop said had any effect; he was forced to perform the ceremony. He pressed the crown upon Elise's head so tightly that she was blinded by pain. But how much greater was her grief for her brothers!

She was pledged not to speak, yet as the days passed she yearned to confide in the king, who loved her and wanted so much to please her. Each night when he was sleeping, Elise stole away into her chamber and knitted one tunic after another. But as she began the seventh she found there was no flax left.

The nettles she required grew only in the churchyard, and she knew she must gather them herself. One moonlit night she stole away fearfully and walked there alone through the empty streets. On the newly dug graves she saw a group of lamias clawing at the earth with long bony fingers. As Elise watched they took up the corpses and devoured the flesh. Her mind was reeling in horror, but she tried to think only of her task.

In all the city only the archbishop had been awake to see her. Now he was certain. The queen was a witch, and it was his duty to tell the king immediately.

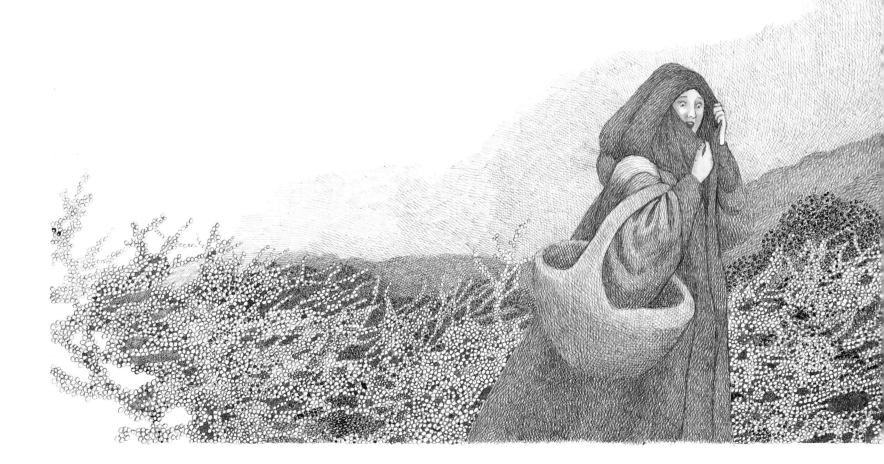

As the king listened to the man's words doubt entered his heart for the first time. He slept restlessly and noticed that Elise got up each night and disappeared into her chamber. Elise saw his sorrow, and it troubled her greatly, adding to the pain she already suffered for her brothers.

But now she had almost finished her task. Only a single tunic remained. Once more, just this once, she must go to the churchyard. She shuddered, thinking of the hideous lamias, but her will was strong.

Silently she went upon her journey, and behind her came the king and the archbishop. They saw her go through the iron gates; they saw the lamias sitting upon the graves. But the king could watch no longer. He imagined she was among them—she whom he had cradled in his arms that evening.

"Let the people judge her," he said. And the people declared she must die by fire.

Elise was led away to a dark dungeon. All she had to lie upon was her bundle of nettles and the tunics she had knitted. Yet they could have given her nothing more precious. She started her work again while urchins mocked her from the street below.

Then toward evening she heard the beating of swans' wings. It was her youngest brother. He had found her at last! Elise rejoiced. Though she might soon be dead, her task was almost done and her brothers were nearby.

All night long she worked. The little mice ran across the floor, dragging the nettles to her, and a bluebird sang sweetly to give her courage.

Shortly before daybreak the eleven brothers came to the palace and demanded to be taken before the king. They begged and threatened until finally the king himself appeared to find out what the tumult meant. But at that very moment the sun came up, and only eleven wild swans were to be seen, flying over the palace.

It was time for the execution. All the people of the city streamed from the gates to see the witch die. Elise was taken to the pyre in an open cart, drawn by a wretched horse. In her hands she twined the green flax. The ten tunics lay at her feet, and she was completing the eleventh.

"Look at the witch," jeered the mob. "She's holding her ugly sorcery. Take it from her! Tear it into pieces!" But just as they rushed at her, eleven swans flew down upon the cart, beating their wide wings.

The crowd moved back fearfully. "Perhaps this is a sign from heaven. Perhaps she is innocent!" some of them whispered.

As the executioner took Elise by the hand she quickly threw the eleven tunics over the wild swans. Suddenly eleven comely young men stood there. No one in the crowd doubted that they were princes, but the youngest had a swan's wing in place of one arm, for Elise had not time enough to finish the sleeve of his tunic.

"Now I dare speak!" she cried. "I am innocent." Then she swayed and fell into her brothers' arms, exhausted by the ordeal she had endured.

"Yes, she is innocent," said the eldest brother, and he told them all that had happened. As he spoke the air was filled with perfume, for every stake in the pyre had grown leaves and red roses. At the very top shone a single white rose. The king picked it and held it to Elise's face. Smelling the fragrance, she awoke and smiled at him where he knelt among her brothers. She had loved him from the beginning but now at last she was at peace.

Then great flocks of birds appeared and followed them back to the palace, and churchbells rang out through all the land.